JUV
FIC

Robinson, Nancy K.

The ghost of
Whispering Rock.

$13.95

| DATE | | | |
|---|---|---|---|
| | | | |
| | | | |
| | | | |
| | | | |
| | | | |
| | | | |
| | | | |
| | | | |
| | | | |
| | | | |
| | | | |
| | | | |

# THE GHOST OF WHISPERING ROCK

# THE GHOST OF WHISPERING ROCK

Nancy K. Robinson

drawings by Ellen Eagle

Holiday House/New York

To Natalie and Norris,
my mother and father

Library of Congress Cataloging-in-Publication Data
Robinson, Nancy K.
   The ghost of Whispering Rock / by Nancy K. Robinson : drawings by
Ellen Eagle.
     p.   cm.
   Summary: While spending the summer after fourth grade at her
family's cabin in the woods, Amy copes with the visit of the bored
and spoiled Erika by inventing a story about a local ghost.
   ISBN 0-8234-0944-9
   [1. Ghosts—Fiction. 2. Country life—Fiction.]   I. Eagle,
Ellen, ill.   II. Title.
PZ7.R56754Gh     1992     92-52856     CIP     AC
[Fic]—dc20

# CONTENTS

*Chapter One*

# The Guest

Every summer vacation, Amy went with her mother and father to a cabin on a wooded hillside high above a pond. There were no other children nearby, but that never bothered Amy.

"You need someone to play with—some-one your own age," her mother said. But Amy was always busy. The days went by so fast, she never had time to do every-thing she meant to do.

Amy wanted to know the name of every

single tree, plant, and wildflower. She kept a nature log and drew pictures of the leaves, flowers, and insects.

Amy had just finished the third grade and she already knew what she was going to be when she grew up. She was going to be a naturalist and live in the woods. If she decided to get married, her husband would have to be a naturalist too.

During the school year, Amy lived in the city. Her small bedroom had only one window that faced on an airshaft. It was always dark. Her apartment building was on a busy corner. All day and all night she could hear noisy traffic and the screaming of sirens.

But up at the cabin she awoke to sunlight and the songs of birds. From the window in her attic room she could see through the white pines and down to the pond where the morning mist rose.

In the evening she listened to the frogs and crickets and fell asleep to the sound of the night wind creeping through the trees.

"This year things will be different," her mother told her one night early in June. She was standing in the doorway of Amy's small bedroom holding a letter. It was a hot night, and the air was filled with the constant sound of sirens.

"What do you mean?" Amy wanted her summer at the cabin to be exactly the same as it had always been.

"Sylvia and John Piker are sending Erika to visit us up at the cabin for a week. They are moving back east. Sylvia needs some time to fix up their new apartment before Erika starts school. Erika has never spent any time in the country. Sylvia thinks it would be good for her."

Amy could not remember Erika. Erika had been her best friend when she was little. The Pikers had lived in the apartment next door.

"You and Erika were always together. You were like sisters," her mother said.

For years Amy had heard how well she and Erika had played together. She had also heard about all the naughty things they had done.

"I'll never forget the day you and Erika used building blocks to make a swimming pool in our bedroom," her father said. "You filled it up with pail after pail of water from the bathtub faucet. The floor has never looked the same."

Amy had seen pictures of herself and Erika as babies. Erika was a mischievous-looking baby. There was a picture of Erika hugging Amy. She had straight white-blond hair that looked as if it had been cut with a bowl over her head. She was hugging Amy's neck.

"Choking me," Amy thought, but her mother had written "Forever friends!" next to the photograph.

"You were miserable when Erika and her family moved away."

"How old was I?"

"Four. You were both four years old, and every night you asked when Erika would be coming back. You included her in your

5

games, almost like an imaginary friend. You even wrote her a letter when you first learned to write."

Amy was beginning to enjoy the idea of a visit from someone who knew nothing about the country. It would be such fun to introduce Erika to nature.

"But I won't act like a teacher," Amy told herself. "I won't lecture her."

They would explore the woods together. Amy would show Erika the beavers building a dam and the baby deer playing at the pond at sunset. At night they could study the stars and constellations.

One day Amy might even take Erika on a picnic to her favorite spot—the ruins of an old stone schoolhouse at Whispering Rock.

But only if Erika could be trusted to keep it a secret.

*Chapter Two*

# Erika Unpacks

Amy spent the first two weeks at the cabin getting ready for her guest. She fixed up the attic room with a cot for Erika and put nature posters on the wall.

The cabin had belonged to her grandfather, who had died before she was born. There was a small library of field guides to nature and an old chest full of jigsaw puzzles and games—old-fashioned games like Chinese checkers, Parcheesi, and darts. There would be plenty to do on a rainy day.

Amy stacked two red plastic milk crates

between the cot and the bed. In the crates she arranged a little library of field guides for Erika to read at night.

After much thought she decided not to put the *Field Guide to Insects and Spiders* in the temporary bookshelf. Spiders gave some people the creeps until they got used to them.

On Tuesday afternoon they went to pick Erika up at the 4:30 bus.

Erika still had white-blond hair cut in the shape of a bowl, but she was wearing a shocking-pink plastic headband. Erika was tall and skinny and very pale. She did not look mischievous anymore. She looked bored and unhappy. Amy had a feeling this trip had not been Erika's idea.

Erika looked Amy up and down without much interest. She seemed uncomfortable when Amy's mother gave her a hug.

Amy had picked a bunch of wildflowers. She handed them to Erika.

Erika mumbled, "Get those away from me. I'm allergic." Amy had to throw them away.

8

## Erika Unpacks

Amy's parents were surprised Erika had brought two large suitcases just for one week. She had also brought a cardboard box filled with food.

"I brought my own," Erika said. "There are a lot of things I don't eat."

"I see." Amy's mother sounded slightly annoyed. She had bought special treats for Erika's visit.

On the way to the cabin Erika sat in the car and read a copy of TV guide.

"How was the bus ride?" Amy's mother asked.

Erika did not answer.

"How are your parents doing?" her mother asked.

There was no response. Then Amy noticed that the shocking-pink headband Erika was wearing had earphones attached. She could hear tinny music.

"She can't hear you," Amy whispered to her mother. "I think she's listening to a tape."

Erika flipped through the TV guide. "The programs come on at different times around here," Erika muttered, "and you don't even get *Stranger Than Fiction* or *Police Files*."

"Are you talking about TV programs?" Amy asked.

Erika didn't say anything. Amy tapped her arm. "There is no television in the cabin," Amy said loudly.

Erika lifted her earphone off one ear. "Huh?"

"No TV," Amy repeated.

Erika's mouth fell open. She stared at Amy.

"You're joking, right?"

Amy shook her head.

A look of panic crossed Erika's face. She looked out the window for the first time. They had just turned onto a dirt road. They passed an old stone wall with a meadow beyond it. There were no houses in sight.

"Where are we anyway?" Erika asked.

Amy saw her parents glance at one another.

"Are we almost there?" Erika asked.

"Because as soon as we get there, I have to call my mother and tell her what programs to tape. I can't miss a whole week of TV."

Amy's mother turned around. "Erika," she said, "there is no telephone in the cabin."

Erika stared at Amy's mother.

"But you *have* to have a telephone. Everybody has a telephone."

Amy's mother sighed. "When we park the car at the base of the hill, you can use the telephone at our neighbors', the McTavys'. I gave your mother the number there. That's how people reach us in an emergency. I'm sure your mother would like to hear that you arrived safely."

Erika shrugged, took out a ballpoint pen and began checking off the programs in the TV guide that she wanted her mother to tape.

Amy sat on the cot in the attic room and watched Erika unpack. Erika had already made it clear that she was going to sleep in the bed and Amy would have to sleep in the cot.

Suddenly Erika stopped what she was doing and pulled off her earphone. "What's that noise?"

"It's an owl." Amy went to the window. "A barred owl. We might be able to see it from here. It's beautiful. Its feathers are so soft it can swoop down on its prey without making a sound."

Erika said, "How fascinating. Will I be tested on that?" and she opened her other suitcase.

Amy watched Erika unpack her tapes and handheld battery-operated video games. She had brought enough video games to entertain herself for a few months. At the bottom of the suitcase were stacks of comic books.

*Weird Tales* was one. *Terrors from the Grave* was another. On the cover there was a bony bluish hand sticking out of the earth.

Amy looked away quickly. She stared

out the window at the white pine trees. She was sure she would not be able to sleep in the same room as those horror comics.

Erika was now busy pulling the field guides out of the milk crates and stuffing them under the bed.

Amy looked at her watch. Only twenty minutes had passed since they got to the cabin. She found herself wondering how many more minutes Erika would be staying.

*Chapter Three*

# Storm Warnings

"It might be a good idea if you wore socks and long pants," Amy's mother said.

Erika was wearing shorts and sandals. Her legs and ankles were already covered with mosquito bites.

"I never wear socks," Erika said coldly. "Up here you will wear socks," Amy's mother said. "There's poison ivy around."

That night Amy's father cooked hot dogs and corn on the cob on a grill. Erika said she did not like to eat outdoors. "I don't really enjoy the mixture of food and dirt," she said. She made herself a peanut-butter-and-jelly sandwich, cut the crusts off the bread, and spent the evening on the screened porch with her handheld video set. It had a small color screen and a loud soundtrack.

Amy and her parents sat on the wooden steps of the cabin and roasted marshmallows over the fire.

The noise of laser guns, whizzing missiles, monsters, and explosions filled the night.

"Sounds like a battlefield," Amy's father grumbled. "The crickets can't even hear themselves think."

Amy had trouble going to sleep that night. Erika stayed up late, chewing bubble gum, listening to tapes, scratching her mosquito bites, and reading her comic books.

She mumbled out loud as she read. Sometimes Amy would catch whole sentences: " 'Hmm, a werewolf would not do that . . . unless. . . .' " Erika made a slight slurping noise, licked her fingertip, and turned the page. " 'unless he were killed

16

by a vampire *and* a werewolf . . . stalking the countryside together.' "

At other times Amy just heard a few words here and there—words like "corpse," "bloody," and "fangs."

Erika finally fell asleep with the light on, snoring delicately.

Amy lay in bed afraid to turn off the light, wishing she had not seen the cover of *Terrors from the Grave* with that bony bluish hand sticking out of the earth.

For breakfast Erika ate Rice Krispies out of a box while everyone else had blueberry pancakes and sausages. She spoke only once.

She asked Amy how she could stand to eat sausages. "You know they're made of the insides of animals—the intestines and liver and things like that."

Amy began to feel a little sick.

"What do you two want to do today?" Amy's mother asked. "Your father and I were going to take a rowboat out on the pond and do some fishing."

"Not me," Erika said at once.

Amy suggested a picnic.

"I already told you I don't like to eat out-doors," Erika said.

"A nature hike?" Amy asked.

"How amusing," Erika muttered. She was playing a video game called Galaxy Raider.

Amy went to tell her parents she couldn't get Erika to do anything.

"We'll take you both down to the pond for a swim after lunch," her father said. "Maybe Erika will feel more interested in exploring after she gets used to the woods a little."

But the swim was not very successful. Erika took two steps into the water and turned back. "It's too cold," she said, "and there's goo on the bottom—goo and slime. I only like to swim in pools." She sat on a towel and read *Haunted Tales*.

"Are you sure you don't want to come out in the rowboat?" Amy's father asked Erika.

Erika shook her head and kept reading.

Amy's mother gave Amy a sympathetic look. "We'll meet you at the cabin," she said.

As soon as the rowboat was out of sight, Erika said, "Let's go back," and she took off her socks.

"It's a good idea to wear socks," Amy said.

"Don't tell me what to do," said Erika.

When they were halfway up the path, Erika announced that she had left her watch down at the pond. "I can't lose that watch," she said. "I'm going back."

Amy stayed behind and waited. Five minutes went by. Ten minutes. She saw a flash of lightning.

Amy ran down the path to help Erika look for her watch.

There was a roll of thunder. The wind was blowing the leaves upside down. The water on the pond was choppy. Amy could see her mother and father rowing back in a hurry. A storm was coming in.

Erika was not down at the pond.

# Chapter Four

# Missing

The sky turned dark. There was a crash of thunder. Large raindrops began to fall.

Amy ran down to the shore to meet her parents. They were dragging the rowboat onto the beach.

"Have you seen Erika?" Amy asked.

Her mother turned and stared at her. "Isn't she with you?"

Suddenly the rain came down in sheets. In a few seconds they were all drenched.

It was such a heavy downpour that the shoreline was invisible. They tried calling

Erika's name, but it did no good. She would not have been able to hear them anyway over the noise of the storm. The wind snapped branches off the trees. There was a violent bolt of lightning.

"That came awfully close," Amy's mother said.

"You two better go back to the cabin," her father said. "Erika's probably there."

"But she couldn't have gotten past me," Amy said. "I would have seen her."

"She might have tried to take a shortcut through the woods," her father said. "I'll have a look."

Amy didn't move. She didn't want her father going off alone in the storm.

"C'mon Amy," her mother said. "Daddy will be all right."

The path was wet and muddy. Amy saw her mother slip on a rock and fall. She scrambled to her feet again, but she was limping. "I think I did something to my ankle," she muttered.

When the cabin came into view, Amy prayed, "Erika, please be there!"

Erika was not at the cabin.

Amy's mother took off her shoe and sock and collapsed onto the couch. Her ankle was swollen and bruised. Her face was pale.

"I'll go tell Daddy she's not here," Amy said.

"No," said her mother. "Stay here. We should both wait here."

A half hour went by. Her mother soaked her foot in a pan of water, but it swelled up even more.

Amy was sure something had happened to her father.

Finally she heard his footsteps on the porch. She ran to meet him. He was so wet and cold, his lips were blue.

"No sign of her?" he asked.

Amy shook her head. "And Mommy hurt her ankle."

"Don't worry," her mother called. "It's probably just a bad bruise. I'm all right."

Her father came inside. He was shivering.

Amy's mother looked up at him. "I think we should report Erika missing right now.

I don't think we should wait. This storm could go on for hours."

Her father nodded. "I'll go down to the McTavys' cabin and call the police."

"I'll go with Daddy," Amy said quickly. "I can tell them what she was wearing."

But when Amy and her father got to the McTavys' cabin, the telephone was already in use.

Erika was talking to her mother long-distance.

It was a cozy scene. Erika was curled up on a rocking chair in front of the fireplace with the telephone on her lap. There was a cup of cocoa with marshmallows on a small table beside her.

"She's been on the phone for almost an hour," Mrs. McTavy whispered. "I assumed you knew where she was. She seemed so upset, I thought a nice hot drink might be good for her."

Amy and her father stood in the doorway dripping wet.

Erika didn't turn around. "No! I'm not

staying another day!" she told her mother. "I hate it here." She paused and listened for a moment.

"I already told you! There's nothing to do. There's no TV. Amy is boring. The whole family is boring. They try to make me do these stupid things. . . ."

Finally she grumbled, "All right. I'll call you tomorrow, but I'm not going to change my mind."

Erika got up and stretched. She seemed neither surprised nor embarrassed to see Amy and her father. "Mom said I could come home tomorrow if I still feel the same way," Erika told them.

"And do you still feel bored?" Amy's father asked politely.

"Bored out of my mind," Erika assured him.

"Well, it's a funny thing," Amy's father said softly. "We haven't been bored. In fact, we've had a rather exciting afternoon thanks to you. Would you like to hear about it?"

26

## Chapter Five

# Cabin Fever

"Your father's mean," Erika told Amy that night.

"He's not mean," Amy said. "He just said you had to let people know where you were going."

"And I don't like these new rules," Erika went on. "I don't see why I can't play video games downstairs or on the porch."

"He doesn't like the noise," Amy said. "Neither does my mother. Neither do I."

"Then don't listen," Erika snapped.

Erika was in a rotten mood. She was all packed except for the towel she was using. She couldn't wait to leave. Amy couldn't wait to get rid of her.

That night Erika mumbled her way through *Ghostly Terrors*. Amy stayed awake for hours wondering if the cabin were haunted by her grandfather's ghost.

But Erika couldn't leave the next day. It had rained all night. It was still raining. There had been a lot of flooding. Roads were washed out. They couldn't even get Erika down to the bus stop.

Amy's mother's ankle was still swollen.

"I'll go into the clinic tomorrow if it's not better," she said. Her father had caught a bad cold. They spent the day sleeping and reading by the fireplace in the main room of the cabin.

Amy and Erika were trapped together in the attic.

Erika had no interest in playing Chinese checkers or Parcheesi. She groaned when Amy suggested doing a jigsaw puzzle. She

lay on her side on the bed playing Galaxy Raider over and over.

Amy had always loved the sound of the rain on the cabin roof, but not now—not with the background noise of electronic warfare.

"Couldn't you stop for a little while?" she asked Erika.

"What do you expect me to do?" Erika asked crossly. "I've run out of comics."

Amy glanced at *Ghostly Terrors* lying at the end of the bed.

"Can we throw them out?" she asked.

"Why?" Erika asked.

"I don't know. I thought since you were finished reading them . . ."

Erika was looking at her. She looked at *Ghostly Terrors*. "Do they frighten you?" she asked.

"Of course not," Amy said. "I just don't find them particularly . . . um . . . attractive. You know, blood and guts and stuff like that."

"You're scared of them," Erika said.

"I'm not," Amy said angrily. "They're childish and ridiculous. Look at that ghost."

Amy pointed to the greenish-white wisp on the cover and tried not to shiver. It had black hollows for eyes and a skeleton mouth. "It's totally unrealistic," she said.

"Unrealistic?" Suddenly Erika was interested. "How do you know?" she asked. "Have you ever met a real ghost?"

"Once," Amy said casually.

"Where?" Erika asked.

"Oh, right around here," Amy said. "Near Whispering Rock."

"Whispering Rock?" Erika breathed. "Oh, I love that name. Where is it? Tell me. Tell me what happened."

To Amy's amazement Erika shut off the video handset and sat up waiting for Amy to go on. Her eyes were bright. There was a little color in her cheeks. She looked like her baby pictures. "Tell me!" she said.

There wasn't much to tell, but Amy figured she'd make the most of it.

"Well, I was walking one afternoon up on the trail toward Whispering Rock. I looked into the forest, and I saw something white and transparent flitting up into the trees. At first I thought it was the mist rising . . ."

"And then?" Erika asked.

Amy was quiet. If she told Erika the truth, the story would be over in one sentence: "And that's exactly what it was— the mist rising."

But instead she said, "I'm not sure I want to talk about it."

Erika was all sympathy. She seemed to have respect for someone who had had a real encounter with the supernatural. "Try," she said kindly. "It might help to tell someone."

"Maybe later," Amy said.

Erika suddenly said, "You know, if these comic books really bother you, I can throw them out. I've never had a direct experience myself, but I can imagine what it feels like."

Amy shrugged. "It's up to you, but it is a little hard to be around that fake baby stuff when you've actually seen the real thing."

"I understand," Erika murmured. "I'll throw them out."

For the rest of the afternoon the two girls were quiet. They lay on their beds listening to the wind and the rain. Erika fell asleep for a while, but Amy amused herself by trying to think up a simple, elegant little ghost story to entertain her guest.

## Chapter Six

# The Ghost of Whispering Rock

"You don't have to talk about it," Erika said when they were getting ready for bed, "but since I'll be leaving tomorrow, I just thought . . . well, I was wondering . . . when did you first realize it wasn't just the mist?"

"I thought it was the mist, so I kept going," Amy said.

"And when you looked back?" Erika asked.

"I didn't look back," Amy said.

"But you heard something, right?"

"Well, it was the strangest thing . . ." Amy said slowly. "As soon as I caught sight of Whispering Rock, a shadow seemed to pass over the landscape. The wind died down and everything was still. The birds stopped singing. There were no forest noises at all—not even the stream murmuring down below."

Erika gasped. "And that's when you turned around and saw it, right?"

"Well, no," Amy said. Erika's questions were contributing so much to the suspense that Amy decided to go very slowly. "That's when I felt something behind me. A Presence. I started to run. I figured once I got to Whispering Rock, I would be safe. I would hide in the ruins of the old schoolhouse right behind it."

"But you can't really hide from a Presence, can you?" Erika asked.

"No, you can't," Amy said, "but I didn't know that at the time."

She would have to change her story!

"They never have those in comic books," Erika said sadly. "I guess they think a Presence is too scary for kids."

"And very hard to draw," Amy agreed. "Look, Erika, I'm getting tired talking about this all at once. Do you mind if I tell you the rest tomorrow?"

Amy hadn't the faintest idea where the story was going. She was extremely tired. She hadn't had much sleep for the past two nights. And now that the room was free of those horror comics . . .

"Just tell me one more thing," Erika begged. "Why is it called Whispering Rock?"

"No one really knows," Amy said.

Amy knew perfectly well why it was called Whispering Rock since she herself had named it. When she sat on the rock, she could hear the whispering of the leaves on the trees in the forest below. But that didn't sound very interesting.

"I know!" Erika suddenly said. "Maybe it's called Whispering Rock because you

can hear the whispers of the schoolchildren of long ago—the children who went
to that school."

Amy was delighted with that.

"By any chance," Erika went on, "did
anything violent happen in that schoolhouse—a murder, a wicked schoolmas-
ter—anything like that?" Her eyes were
shining.

Amy studied Erika and thought what a
helpful listener she was. If Amy just con-
tinued to let Erika drag the story out of
her, there would be quite a nice little ghost
story by the time they were finished. Erika
probably deserved half the credit.

"Very little is known about the history of
that schoolhouse," Amy began, "but now
that you mention it, that figure could have
been a schoolteacher."

"What figure?" Erika asked.

"I looked up and saw that same misty
shape sort of slithering over Whispering
Rock. It began to take the form of a human
figure—a man . . . um . . . a man in an

old-fashioned tweed jacket with leather patches on the sleeves. . . ."

(Was she overdoing it?)

"A schoolteacher," Erika said promptly.

"Maybe," Amy said. "Then I saw the eyes."

"The eyes?"

Amy nodded and went on in a faraway voice. "Yes, I suppose it was the eyes that bothered me most. They had this strange fiery red glow in the middle . . ."

Erika caught her breath.

"Nice touch," Amy thought, but she reminded herself once again to keep it simple.

"I wonder," Erika said, "if it was the type of ghost that is seeking revenge. There are many types of ghosts, you know. They usually have some purpose for being in a certain place. They don't just hang out."

"How interesting." Amy did not want to hear any more. She wanted to wrap up the story as fast as she could.

"All at once the figure disappeared. The sun came out. The birds sang. The stream

39

murmured down below. Everything was back to normal."

"How many minutes had gone by since you first sensed that Presence?" Erika wanted to know.

"I'm not sure," Amy said. "I had a feeling that quite a lot of time had passed."

"Time lapse." Erika nodded wisely. "That often happens in a sighting." She reached over and turned off the light. "That's quite an experience you had," she said. "Thanks for telling me."

Amy was proud. "I hope I didn't scare you," she said. "Maybe I shouldn't have told you about those eyes."

"Oh, the eyes don't scare me," Erika said. "That kind of thing never does."

"Well, they scare me," Amy muttered. She was beginning to wish she had left that part out. She couldn't stop thinking about those eyes with their fiery red glow.

"Of course they scare you," Erika said gently, "because it really happened to you."

Amy's heart was beating fast. "That Presence scares me too," she admitted.

"I wish something scary like that would happen to me," Erika said. "The only thing that ever scares me is hearing my parents fighting all night in these really low voices."

Amy wasn't paying attention. All she could think about was that misty shape slithering up Whispering Rock.

"They don't fight so much when I'm around," Erika said in a sleepy voice. "That's another reason I have to go back tomorrow."

Amy's eyes opened wide. She had completely forgotten that Erika was leaving the next day.

She was going to be alone in this room every night . . .

for the rest of the summer . . .

living with the terrifying ghost story she had invented herself.

41

*Chapter Seven*

# The Picnic

It was a few minutes after midnight.

Amy got out of bed and put her mouth right next to Erika's ear. "Are you still awake?" she asked.

Erika had been snoring peacefully for hours. She awoke with a start. "What's the matter?"

"I made it up," Amy said. "I made up the whole story. There is no Ghost of Whispering Rock."

"Good story," Erika murmured, and she went back to sleep.

## The Picnic

Amy crawled into bed and waited for the terror to subside. Now that she had confessed, she was sure the story would no longer seem real.

She woke up before dawn in a cold sweat. She buried her face in her pillow and burst into tears.

"Now what?" Erika asked sleepily.

"I dreamt about Whispering Rock," Amy sobbed, "and that misty shape . . ."

Erika reached over and turned on the light. "I thought you said the story wasn't true."

". . . and now, I've ruined my favorite spot in the whole world. I can never go back there!"

"Of course you can," Erika said. "In fact you have to—so you can see there is no ghost."

"But what if there *is* a ghost?"

"That would be interesting too," Erika said, but when she saw the look on Amy's face, she added, "in a different way, of course."

*     *     *

"Don't you see," Erika said at breakfast. "The only way to get that story out of your mind is to go there right now—this morning—with me."

It was a beautiful day. Amy was feeling a little better. "Well, maybe," she said.

Amy's father was taking her mother to the clinic to have her ankle looked at. He told Erika they would be back in plenty of time to get her to the one o'clock bus.

"And we certainly wouldn't want you to miss it," Amy's mother said. "That is . . . I mean . . ." She looked helplessly at Amy's father who simply muttered. "Don't worry, she'll be on that bus."

As soon as they were gone, Erika said, "Well?"

"I suppose we could go," Amy said. "We could take a picnic, maybe pick some blue-berries . . ." Then she remembered that Erika hated picnics.

To her surprise Erika said, "That's an excellent idea. We'll just behave as if everything's perfectly normal. You know, two regular-type kids on a hike, enjoying nature, and having a harmless picnic on an ordinary old rock. Before you know it, you'll forget what really happened there."

"But nothing did happen," Amy said.

"Oh yeah, I forgot," Erika said. She looked so disappointed, Amy giggled.

"We'll have to leave my parents a note," Amy said.

"I'll write the note," Erika said. "You make the picnic."

Amy and Erika had a wonderful morning up at Whispering Rock. Erika had never seen highbush blueberries before. She ate one for every one she picked, but somehow managed to fill up the pail.

"Do you think I can bring some home to my mother?" Erika asked. "She makes pies."

"Of course," Amy said.

They sat on Whispering Rock, which was right next to the doorway of the abandoned schoolhouse.

"I think I do hear the whispers of school-children," Erika said. "I'll bet those kids sat here and talked behind the teacher's back."

The sun was so hot they decided to have their picnic in the old stone schoolhouse. It was cool and dark inside. The windows had once been boarded up for years and were covered with heavy metal bars. They each sat at an old wooden desk. Amy opened the lid of the picnic basket.

"Wait a minute," she said. "Where's the pail of blueberries?"

"I left it right outside," said Erika.

"In the sun?" Amy groaned. "They'll be cooked!"

Luckily the pail was standing in a small shadow cast by Whispering Rock. But Amy knew the sun would soon be directly overhead. There would be no shade. She decided to bring the blueberries inside.

As she was bending over to pick up the pail, she saw a shape on the rock. She stopped.

"Don't run," she told herself, "*and leave the blueberries where they are.*"

Without even straightening up, she moved backward through the doorway as quickly and quietly as she could.

"What did you see out there?" Erika wanted to know. "There's something on Whispering Rock, right?"

Amy opened her mouth, but she couldn't speak.

"What is it?" Erika demanded. Then she said, "I'll have a look."

"Don't go out there," Amy said hoarsely.

"I'll just peek around the doorway," Erika said.

Amy grabbed Erika's arm and held onto her. "Stay away from there!" she said. "I don't think it saw me, but it may have sensed my presence."

"Does it have reddish eyes?" Erika asked.

Amy nodded and kept her own eyes fixed on the ground outside the doorway. She was trembling.

"Is it slithering over the rock?" Erika asked.

"Not right this minute." Amy's voice seemed to be choking her. "But I . . . I . . . recognize the type."

Erika's eyes had gotten very big. "Is it the type that seeks revenge?"

Amy nodded. "No question about that," she said, "but there is also a danger that it will strike first. Look," she said, "the most important thing to remember in a situation like this is to remain calm."

"I'm calm," Erika said. "I'd be even more calm if you'd just let me take a peek. It's scarier for me not to see something. That's just the way I am."

Amy took a firm hold of Erika's arm. "Erika, don't you understand? It's on the rock. The rock is less than three feet away from that doorway. Now be quiet for a moment and let me think."

Erika was quiet. She never took her eyes off Amy. Finally she said, "Can I ask just one little tiny question?"

Amy sighed. "Go ahead. Maybe it will help me think."

"What about the jacket? Is it wearing a tweed jacket?"

Amy couldn't figure out what in the world Erika was talking about.

"Why would a snake wear a tweed jacket?" she asked.

"Especially on such a hot day," Erika agreed. She was quiet again. Then she said, "Did you say *a snake*?"

"Well, what do you think I was talking about," Amy asked crossly. "It's a copperhead. I'm sure of it."

*Chapter Eight*

# A Quick Lesson in Nature

"They have hollow fangs in the front of the upper jaw," Amy explained. "The venom is in there."

"Venom is poison, right?" Erika asked.

Amy nodded. "I knew there were copperheads around here, but there hasn't been a sighting for seventeen years. They are very shy snakes."

"Do you think it's feeling shy now?" Erika asked. Her eyes were fixed on the ground outside the door.

"It's coiled up sunning itself," Amy said.

"Asleep?" Erika asked.

"I don't know," Amy said.

"Well, were its eyes closed?"

"Snakes don't sleep with their eyes closed. They don't have eyelids," Amy said.

"Did it see you?" Erika asked.

"I don't know."

"Can it hear us talking?"

"Snakes don't really hear, but I think they can feel sound vibrations through their skull bones."

Amy was grateful to Erika for her questions; they helped her remember her *Field Guide to North American Snakes*.

"A copperhead is a pit viper," she went on. "Pit vipers have heat detectors—these little holes between the nostril and the eyes. They can sense their prey even in the dark."

"Will it come in here?"

Amy looked around at the barred windows. There was no way of blocking the entrance. They were trapped. "I don't know," she said.

A moment later she remembered another line from the guide book. " 'In the summer the copperhead is nocturnal.' That means it only hunts at night."

"Hunts for what?" Erika asked.

"Birds, lizards, mice, rats. . . . Sometimes it comes looking in basements or deserted dark places."

"Amy," Erika said slowly, "by any chance, would this be the perfect place?"

Amy nodded.

Erika said, "Well, if it comes in here, we'll just kill it."

"I think we're safer if we hold still," Amy said. "They usually don't strike unless they're stepped on or surprised. Besides, I don't even know how to kill a snake."

"We'll get some rocks," Erika suggested. "I'll go outside and. . . ." She stopped. "No I won't."

\* \* \*

At quarter to one, Erika said, "I'm going to miss the bus."

At one o'clock, she said, "I missed it."

"Well, at least we know my parents will be looking for us now. It takes a while to get up here," Amy said, "but the minute either one of us sees them on the path, we yell, 'Stop! Don't move. There's a copperhead on the rock!' "

Erika practiced that.

At one-thirty Amy said, "Where did you put the note?"

"Right on the door. Don't you remember?" Erika looked at Amy. "Maybe your mother and father were delayed at the clinic. Maybe they just found the note."

But it didn't make sense to Amy. Her parents should have been here by now.

"I'm hungry," Erika said. "Will the snake smell the food and come in?"

Amy was hungry too.

"I don't think copperheads are interested in peanut-butter-and-jelly sandwiches." She opened the basket and handed Erika her sandwich.

Erika looked at the sandwich with disgust. "You left the crusts on," she said. "I never eat crusts."

"You'll eat them now," Amy said quietly. "No crumbs. No garbage. Garbage attracts the rats and mice that copperheads come looking for."

Erika ate the crusts first.

"Erika," Amy said suddenly. "What did you write in the note?"

Erika shrugged. "I told them where we were going."

"What did you say?" Amy asked. "I mean how did you put it?"

"I just said, 'Amy and I went to Whispering Rock on a picnic. We will be back in plenty of time to make my bus.' "

Amy's heart sank. "Didn't you mention the old schoolhouse?" Amy asked.

"No," Erika said. "Why?"

"They'll never know where to look for us," Amy said flatly.

"But it's right there in the note," Erika insisted. "I told them we were going to Whispering Rock."

"It won't mean anything to them." Amy's heart was beating fast. "No one has ever heard of Whispering Rock. I made up the name myself."

## Chapter Nine

# Endings

Neither one of them said anything for quite a long time.

Finally Amy turned to Erika. "There must be some way of finding out if that copperhead is still on the rock."

"Without going outside," Erika agreed.

Amy was quiet. A picture had formed in her mind—a picture of the two of them sitting all night in the pitch dark waiting . . .

Erika suddenly said, "I know the ending!"

# Endings

Amy knew the ending too. A few months from now someone would discover the skeletons of two young girls in the abandoned schoolhouse.

"Listen." Erika was excited. "The figure of the schoolteacher disappears, right? Everything seems normal again . . ."

"Oh *that* story," Amy said.

Erika went on, "You only visit the rock once again with your friend Erika, run into a copperhead, get away safely . . ."

"How?" Amy asked.

"That's beside the point," Erika said. "You just do."

"But how?" Amy wanted to know.

"Shh, you're ruining it. So anyway, you forget about the Ghost of Whispering Rock until one day, years later, you're at the local library getting some books for your daughter who loves ghost stories, and you get to talking with the librarian. 'Do you know anything about that old schoolhouse?' you ask.

"The librarian raises her eyebrows. 'Do

you mean the abandoned schoolhouse by Whipping Rock?'

" 'Whipping Rock? But I used to call it Whispering Rock,' you say, and you tell her about the day you saw this odd figure in a tweed jacket.

"A strange look passes over the librarian's face. 'That was Mr. Craig,' she says. 'He was the cruelest teacher who ever taught at that school. He used to keep his whip on that rock to punish the schoolchildren.'

" 'Does he still live near that old schoolhouse?' you ask.

" 'Oh no, he died over a century ago— long before you were born.' "

"I like that," Amy told Erika, "but there should be a little more." For some reason Amy was finding this relaxing—almost soothing.

There was a rustling sound.

"What was that?" Erika asked.

"Just a mouse or something." Amy was

busy thinking about the ending. Finally she said, "I've got it! I say to the librarian, 'But how did he die?'

" 'As the story goes,' the librarian says, 'he reached for his whip to punish a schoolboy and put his hand on a copperhead who was coiled up on the rock. The copperhead bit him, and he died shortly afterward. Ever since that day, his figure has been seen around that old schoolhouse warning other people to beware of the copperhead.' "

Erika did not seem satisfied. "Wait a minute!" she said. "I think it gets even better—'So there is a Ghost of Whispering Rock,' you say.

" 'There is a Ghost of Whispering Rock,' the librarian answers quietly, 'and some people say it is the ghost of the old schoolteacher. On the other hand . . .'

" 'What?' you ask.

"The librarian looks at you. 'Recently I had a visit from an old friend who is an expert on snakes. He went off exploring, and when he returned, he told me he had come across a copperhead on that rock, but it was a variety that hasn't been seen in these parts for over a hundred years . . .'

" 'Do you mean . . . ?' you ask.

" 'Yes,' she says, 'the very same snake that bit Mr. Craig still haunts that rock. *That* is the Ghost of Whispering Rock.' "

Erika finished the story in a hushed voice.

"Is anyone in there?"

A voice was calling. Both girls jumped.

"Daddy!" Amy screamed. "Watch out! There's a copperhead on the rock right next to you," and she covered her eyes.

There was dead silence. Then she heard her mother's voice. "There he goes. Poor scared thing."

"How did you know where to find us?" Amy asked on the way back.

"I suddenly remembered having picnics up there when I was a child," her mother said, "but I called it Murmuring Rock."

Amy's father looked at his watch. "If we all walk a little faster, I think I'll be able to get Erika to that bus leaving from Fairfield." He turned around. "Now where did she go?"

Amy glanced over her shoulder. Erika was lagging behind.

"Tell her to hurry or we'll miss that one, too," her father said.

Amy went back.

"Look!" Erika was pointing at something on the ground. "I almost didn't see it. It was holding absolutely still, and then suddenly it moved."

Amy looked down. "It's a toad," she said.

"That's what I thought!" Erika said proudly. "I thought it was a toad."

". . . but why can't I stay here longer than a week?" Erika was on the telephone with her mother. "I only have three days left, and the first four don't count."

Amy and her parents were sitting in the McTavys' cabin.

"Mama," Amy whispered. "Please let Erika stay. She promises to wear socks all the time."

"It's a little late for that," her mother said.

"Oh Mom, I forgot to tell you," Erika went on. "I've got poison ivy." Erika was covered with Calamine lotion. "It itches like crazy."

When she got off the phone, her eyes were shining. "I can stay longer than a week if it's all right with you."

Amy's mother smiled. "Of course you can stay. That is, if it's all right . . ." She looked at Amy's father.

Amy's father shrugged. "It's fine with me," he said.

Erika threw her arms around Amy's neck.

"Help!" Amy said. "You're choking me!"